Howie Merton
and the
MAGIC DUST

By Faye Couch Reeves

Illustrated by Jon Buller

A STEPPING STONE BOOK

Random House　New York

To my husband, Ron Reeves,
for believing in magic and me
—F.C.R.

Library of Congress Cataloging-in-Publication Data
Reeves, Faye Couch.
Howie Merton and the magic dust / by Faye Couch Reeves. Illustrated by Jon Buller.
p. cm. "A Stepping Stone book." Summary: A mysterious girl named Eddie tries to make
friends with Howie by promising him magic powers if he follows her orders for a month.
ISBN 0-679-81527-9 (pbk.)—ISBN 0-679-91527-3 (lib. bdg.)
[1. Friendship—Fiction. 2. Magic—Fiction.] I. Title.
PZ7.R2559Ho 1991 [E]—dc20 90-38341

Manufactured in the United States of America 1 2 3 4 5 6 7 8 9 0

Contents

1
Eddie

Howie Merton was in the third grade at Port Amblin Elementary School. He had two missing teeth and a wart on his elbow that all the girls in his class thought was gross. He had a real Spanish coin, too. Best of all, Howie had a dead cat.

Howie liked to scare people. And it was easy with a dead cat. Howie's cat was buried behind the toolshed in the backyard. Howie told everyone that the cat's ghost lived in the toolshed.

"The cat ghost walks by night!" Howie would hiss. "He likes to *jump* on people as they go by." Howie would make a scary face when he said this. It usually worked, especially on easy-to-scare people like his older sister, Sybil. It was really great around

Halloween. On Halloween night Howie and his best friend, Roy, made horrible dead-cat noises from inside the toolshed. They scared a lot of little trick-or-treaters.

Now it was spring, and Howie was taking a shortcut home from school. He cut through five backyards. Then he walked past the toolshed. He and Roy were still the only kids in town who would go past it without running. Howie smiled. He was saving his money to buy paint. He and Roy were going to paint big red cat-paw prints all over the toolshed.

Sybil was in the backyard standing on her head. She was always standing on her head. She was in training. She wanted to be ready if they ever decided to make standing on your head an Olympic event.

"Someday you are going to wake up and find out your head is flat!" Howie said.

Sybil stuck her tongue out at Howie. So did her best friend, Edith.

"If Howie Merton was my brother, I'd leave home," Edith said. She pushed her glasses back into place on her nose.

"If you were my sister, I'd help you pack," said Howie.

Howie went into the house. He was hoping

to find Mrs. Ross in the kitchen. Mrs. Ross worked at the Mertons' house two days a week. She took care of Sybil, Howie, and Lionel, their younger brother, while Mrs. Merton went to work. Not only did she make wonderful dinners for the Mertons, she made cookies, too. In Howie's opinion, Mrs. Ross was the best cookie baker in town.

He found her standing at the sink. "Hi, Mrs. Ross," said Howie. "Are there cookies?"

Mrs. Ross smiled. "Sit down," she said. "I'll get you some."

"How is Miss Marshmallow?" asked Howie. Miss Marshmallow was Mrs. Ross's big fluffy white cat. Whenever Mrs. Ross went on a vacation, Miss Marshmallow stayed with the Mertons.

"My granddaughter Edwina says she's spoiled rotten," said Mrs. Ross. "And she might be right. Miss Marshmallow eats like a horse. She also comes and goes as she pleases. She's here and then she's gone."

Howie held out his empty plate. "Just like the cookies." He tried to look extra hungry.

Mrs. Ross laughed. "No more cookies," she said. "But you'll be happy to know I made your favorite dinner—roast beef. Why don't you change your clothes so you can play for a while?"

"Okay," said Howie. He went upstairs to the bedroom he shared with Lionel. Lionel was in the closet on his hands and knees.

"Don't make a mess, Lionel," Howie said. "I'll have to clean it up." He unbuttoned his school shirt.

Lionel came out of the closet. He was covered with clothes that had fallen off hangers. "I'm not making a mess. Besides, I don't think this room can get much worse. Mrs. Ross says she can't remember if the carpet is blue or brown."

Howie moved a pile of books, a bat, three pairs of jeans, and some candy wrappers. "It's blue," he said, letting everything settle back onto the floor. "What are you doing in the closet anyway?"

"Looking for something for show and tell," said Lionel. He was in kindergarten. He had show and tell every week and he loved it. "Howie, what can I take tomorrow?" he asked. "Stevie Potter brought a real snakeskin in today. And Gloria Nicks says she's bringing a stuffed coyote. I don't have anything good."

"How about the cat that's out by the toolshed? You can take that to school," said Howie. "I could dig it up for you."

Lionel's eyes grew big and round. He was just as scared of the cat ghost as all the other kids. "No, thanks, Howie," he said. "Can you help me find something else?"

Howie chose a pair of jeans from the heap on the floor and pulled them on. "If I help you, there will be a small charge: your new baseball card."

"No way!" said Lionel. "Mom says that brothers should help each other. Besides, you already have my flashlight, my old maid card game, and my compass. And I could have taken the compass for show and tell."

"No payment, no help," Howie said. He went outside to play.

Sybil and Edith were gone. Howie had the backyard to himself. He picked up his basketball and started for the hoop hanging over the garage door. Then he stopped. There was a girl leaning against the toolshed. Her sweater came down below her knees. Her jeans were too big, and they were rolled up at the bottom. She was looking right at Howie.

"So this is the toolshed I've heard so much about," she said. "I don't see any cat ghost paw prints. I don't hear any crying cat ghosts."

Howie frowned at her. "Who are you? What are you doing here?"

She looked at the house. "I'm just coming to see . . ." She stopped. Then she started again. "Uh, I'm just coming to see the Mertons' toolshed. You *are* Howie Merton, aren't you?"

Howie nodded.

"Who buried the dead cat, anyway?" she asked. "Was it you? Or was it Roy, Roy, the Wonder Boy?"

Howie was amazed. He had never seen this girl before. How did she know about the dead cat? How did she know what he called his best friend Roy? "Who *are* you?" he asked again.

The girl smiled. "Call me Eddie," she said.

"Pretty dumb name for a girl," said Howie.

"Oh, I'm not just a girl," Eddie said. She pushed her blond hair out of her eyes. "I'm magic!" She walked away slowly. "See you around—if you don't turn square!"

Howie watched her. "Magic?" he called after her with a laugh. "Sure! You're magic and I'm Superman!" The girl just kept walking. She didn't even turn around.

Howie kept thinking about her. He was thinking about her when his mother came home. He was thinking about her as he waved good-bye to Mrs. Ross. He was thinking about her so much at dinner that he could only eat three helpings of roast beef. His mother felt his head to make sure that he wasn't sick.

2
Magic Trainee

Howie looked for Eddie on his way to school the next day. He looked for her on the playground, too. But she wasn't there.

After school he walked home with Roy. "Do you know a girl named Eddie?" he asked Roy.

"No, but I can sing 'A Boy Named Sue,' " said Roy.

"Ha, ha. But I'm not kidding," said Howie. "I met this girl named Eddie, and she doesn't go to school. I've never seen her before."

"So what? Who cares about some girl anyway? Girls are dumb," Roy said as they came to his house. "See ya!"

Howie walked on. He passed Mrs. Ross's house. She lived next door to Roy. He thought about Eddie. Eddie wasn't like other girls. She didn't believe that there was a cat ghost in the toolshed. Every kid in town believed that story.

Then he saw her. She was standing on the corner.

"Hey, Superman," Eddie said. "Looking for a phone booth?" She was wearing a sweat-shirt that was too big for her.

Howie stopped. "Why don't you go to school?" he asked. *"Everyone* has to go to school."

"I told you, I'm magic. Magic people don't go to school. Everyone knows that."

"If you are magic, you have to prove it to me," said Howie. "Fly around the block. Make my lunchbox disappear."

"I can do lots of magic things," Eddie said. "For example, I know things that no one else knows."

"Like what?" asked Howie.

"Like where you and Roy buried your piggy bank. Like how you and Roy made all those cat ghost sounds last Halloween to scare Sybil and Sandra Sue Baker." Eddie took a breath. "Like that you had roast beef for dinner last night. So there!"

Howie's mouth hung open. This girl knew the most secret secrets that Howie and Roy had! She even knew what he had had for dinner last night!

Howie looked at Eddie's eyes. They were green, like a cat's eyes. Howie had never seen a person with green eyes before. He felt goose bumps under his flannel shirt. Eddie *was* magic. Maybe even a witch!

"I could let you into my club, you know," she said.

Howie swallowed hard. "What club?"

"The *Magic* Club," said Eddie. "You could sort of be a Magic Person in training. A Magic Trainee!" she said as if she had just thought of it. "I could leave notes for you telling you what I want you to do. I could leave them on the door of the toolshed." She smiled. "The home of the cat ghost."

"Why do you have to leave notes?" Howie asked. "Where will you be?"

"Magic is very big right now," said Eddie. "I'm out of town a lot. But that doesn't matter. You just, well, you do everything I tell you to do for—one month! If you do *everything* that I tell you to do for just one month, I'll blow magic dust on you! Yeah," said Eddie. "That's what I'll do! But you've got to follow my orders."

Howie wasn't sure this was a good idea. What if Eddie wanted him to do something his mom and dad didn't like? Or something scary? What if she told him to saw his sister Sybil in half? Howie had seen a man do that on television once. "I wouldn't have to saw anybody in half, would I?" he asked.

Eddie shook her head.

"If I was magic, could I get all the spelling words right every week?" Howie asked. He was the fourth-worst speller in the third grade.

Eddie thought for a moment. She nodded.

"If I was magic, could I talk to Santa? I want to be sure I get a real walkie-talkie this year. I don't want socks or underwear!"

She smiled. "Sure you could! Spelling and walkie-talkies. No problem," she said.

Magic! Howie could see it all now. . . .

Howie "Magic" Merton, hidden deep in the jungle, speaks into his high-power long-range walkie-talkie. "Magic Merton to Roy, Roy, the Wonder Boy. Come in, Wonder Boy. Over."

"Magic!" says Roy. "Is it true that you got one hundred percent on your spelling test again this week? Over."

"No," says Magic. "I got one thousand per-cent. Ms. Jackson said one hundred percent just wasn't high enough for spelling as per-fect as mine. Over."

"Wow," says Roy. "You really *are* magic, Magic."

Howie smiled at Eddie. "What do I have to do?" he asked.

3

Week One:
Fish Heads Really Smell

Early the next morning Howie found a note from Eddie on the door of the toolshed. Eddie might be magic, but her handwriting was terrible.

MAGIC TRAINEE ORDER #1
TODAY YOU WILL MEET THE MAGIC GIVER (EDDIE) BY WATSON'S PRETTY FINE FISH ON BARTLETT STREET. COME RIGHT AFTER SCHOOL. DON'T BE LATE.

Howie had never been to Bartlett Street. It was down by the docks where the fishing boats came in. Howie folded the note and put it in the pocket of his jeans along with his math homework. He went into the kitchen to say good-bye to his mother.

"See ya, Mom," said Howie.

"Are you coming straight home from school this afternoon?" his mother asked.

"No," Howie said quickly. "I'm going to Roy's house." Howie felt strange saying this. It was one thing to make up stories about cat ghosts to scare Sybil, but he knew it was wrong to tell his mother something that wasn't true. He picked up his lunch.

"Well, have a good day, honey," she said. Howie reached up and gave her a hug.

The day seemed to last forever. Howie couldn't wait to get out of school. At the sound of the last bell he raced for the door. He was so fast he even beat Roy. That was fine with Howie. He didn't want to tell Roy about the magic club, at least not yet. He wanted to wait until he was magic and then surprise Roy with his powers.

Howie walked down Main Street and turned on Bartlett Street. Eddie was waiting for him.

She looked at her watch. "You made it just in time," she said. "You were almost late. Since you made it, come with me." Howie followed Eddie down the alley behind Watson's Pretty Fine Fish. The alley ended very close to the docks. Eddie walked over to two baskets that were sitting at the end of the dock.

She picked up one of the baskets. "You get the other one," she said.

Howie leaned over to pick up the basket. It smelled terrible. He looked inside. It was filled with fish heads. "Gross!" he yelled, grabbing his nose. "Why do we have to carry fish heads?"

"Fish heads are good for gardens," said Eddie calmly. "I have a magic friend who needs these fish heads for his compost pile." She picked up her basket and started toward a path that curved up a hill.

Howie just stood there.

"You don't have to come with me," said Eddie. "You don't have to carry fish heads. And you don't have to be magic, either."

Howie picked up the basket and ran to catch up with Eddie. It was hard. The basket was heavy, and he had to walk uphill and hold his breath to keep out the horrible fish smell all at the same time. He was glad when Eddie stopped at the first house on the path.

A very old man answered the door. He had blue eyes and snowy white hair. Maybe he's Santa Claus, thought Howie. And he doesn't have a beard because it's only March. Eddie said that we were going to see a magic friend. Santa is magic. Howie decided to be nice to him just in case.

"Howie, this is Thomas," Eddie told Howie. "Thomas, meet Howie," she said to the man. "Howie wants to be magic—you know—like me!" Eddie seemed to have something in her eye. She blinked and winked. "Howie is going to do *everything* I want him to do for one month. Then he'll be magic!"

Thomas coughed until Eddie had to pound him on the back. "Well," he said to Howie when he could talk again, "I wonder what our friend Eddie will want you to do?"

"Magic friend," Eddie reminded him.

"Oh, yes," said Thomas, "magic friend. Eddie *is* one of the most magical people I know," he said.

"See?" Eddie said to Howie. "Everybody knows that I'm magic. Anyway, we can't stand around here talking all day. We have work to do." Eddie picked up her basket and walked over to a wooden box on the side of Thomas's house. The box was about two feet high. Howie thought it looked like a big sandbox with garbage in it instead of sand. He, Eddie, and Thomas poured the fish heads onto the grass cuttings and food scraps that were already in the box.

"This," Eddie told Howie, "is a compost pile. You put things in it that will help your garden grow, like potato peelings, apple cores—"

"Leftover oatmeal," Thomas added.

"Leftover oatmeal," Eddie agreed, "and fish heads. Nothing is better for plants than fish heads. The Indians knew that!"

Thomas smiled at Howie. "I can see that you are going to be a great help. Eddie is a big help. She runs to the store for me."

She probably flies, thought Howie.

"She weeds my garden," Thomas said. "She is quite a girl. How about a cookie? Mrs. Ross brought me some homemade cookies just this morning."

"Do you know Mrs. Ross too? Our Mrs. Ross?" asked Howie. "How do you know—"

"You go and pour the milk, Thomas," interrupted Eddie. "We'll be right in." Thomas nodded. He walked slowly to the back door.

Eddie turned to Howie. "You have one more thing to do before you are finished for the day." Eddie stepped up onto the edge of the compost box. It was only a couple of inches wide, but she walked easily around the edge. She did not even begin to tip over or fall. How did she do that? Howie wondered.

Eddie jumped to the ground. "Now you do the same thing," she said.

Howie stepped up. He put one foot on the edge of the box. The fish heads stared up at him with their fishy eyes. He looked at Eddie. Her green eyes stared at him, too. Daring him.

"You aren't afraid of a few fish heads, are you?" Eddie asked with a smile. "Or is it the orange peels you're afraid of?" She laughed.

Howie took a deep breath. No girl was going to laugh at him. He slid his foot forward. Then he put his other foot in front. He took a few steps. He was doing all right! He took another step. Then he began to tip. First he tipped one way. Then the other. He tried to stop, but it was too late. He fell right into the oatmeal, the potato peelings, and all those fish heads with their staring fish eyes. He sat in the middle of the fish heads and groaned.

When he crawled out of the compost box, Howie had a potato peel over one ear, a fish head down the front of his shirt, and oat-

meal in both his shoes. Soap and water at
Thomas's house did not help. Thomas made
him eat his cookie outside. Howie decided that
Thomas was not Santa Claus.

Howie's eyes watered all the way home.
With every step he took, the oatmeal in his
shoes squished between his toes. He could
hardly breathe. He smelled just like Miss
Marshmallow's cat food. The neighborhood
cats thought so too. Every few steps Howie
had to stop and yell *"Scat!"* to all the cats that

were following him. They ran away but came right back again.

Finally he was home. Howie opened the front door of his house. If he could just get to the bathroom, he would take a bath—clothes and all. He could hang his clothes up to dry in the basement and no one would know what had happened.

He tiptoed down the hall. He was just two steps away from the bathroom when he heard a terrible howl. Did one of those cats follow him into the house? Howie turned around. It was his mother.

"Howard Merton!" she cried. His mother only called him Howard when she was *really* mad. "What have you done? You smell disgusting!"

Howie tried to think. He didn't want to lie. Not again. "I fell into a compost pile," he said. "It had dead fish in it." He lifted one foot. "Oatmeal, too." Howie closed his eyes and waited for the next question. He would have to tell his mother where and what and why.

"I hope it didn't upset Mrs. Brown," said Mrs. Merton as she started to pull off Howie's shirt.

Mrs. Brown? Of course! Mrs. Brown! She

lived two houses away from Roy. She had a big garden. She must have a compost pile too! Howie took a deep breath. "Mrs. Brown didn't see me fall," he said. That was true. Mrs. Brown hadn't seen him fall.

"All right." Mrs. Merton looked at Howie's shirt with a frown. "Take off the rest of your clothes and give them to me right now. If they go into your bedroom, they may never come out."

Howie took them off and handed them to his mother.

She held his clothes out as far as she could. "Now take a bath!" she said.

Howie walked into the bathroom. Lionel was there looking in the medicine cabinet. "There's nothing good in here for show and tell, Lionel," Howie said. "Unless you want to take the bubble bath."

Lionel stared at Howie. "Wow," he said. "You smell terrible! Worse than Mom's perfume." He handed the bubble bath to Howie. "Here," he said. "You need this more than I do."

Howie sighed. "Thanks, Lionel," he said.

Lionel smiled. "No charge!" he said.

4

Week Two:
Mom's Little Helper

Howie stopped at the toolshed door every day to look for a note from Eddie. He had already marked off five days on his school calendar since he had seen her.

On the afternoon of the sixth day Howie was throwing a basketball in his backyard. He ran to catch a rebound and tripped. He fell flat on his face. When he looked up, he saw a pair of old sneakers. He looked a little farther and saw jeans, rolled up at the bottom.

"You have trouble staying on your feet, don't you, Howie?" Eddie said.

Howie got up slowly. He dusted himself off.

"Don't worry. No more fish heads," said Eddie. She held out a folded piece of paper. Howie didn't take it.

"You aren't going to stop now, are you?" she asked.

"I'm no quitter," Howie said.

"Good," said Eddie. She handed the paper to Howie. "Someone is waiting for me," she said as she turned to go. "Remember, you have to do *everything* the note says. I'll know!" Then she ran past the toolshed and out of sight.

Howie unfolded the paper. It said:

MAGIC TRAINEE ORDER #2
THIS WEEK THE MAGIC TRAINEE (YOU) WILL
DO THE DISHES. YOU WILL CLEAN YOUR
ROOM.

Howie groaned. He hated doing dishes. He also hated cleaning his room. How does she think of these things? Howie wondered.

That night there was ham for dinner. Howie loved ham. He was eating a second helping when he remembered his magic trainee orders. "Mom, I'll wash the dishes tonight," he said.

Mrs. Merton choked on her food. Mr. Merton had to pat her on the back. "You'll do *what?*" asked Mrs. Merton.

"I'll wash dishes tonight," Howie said. He picked up a plate and walked to the sink.

"Temporary insanity," Sybil said.

"It is very nice of you to offer, Howie," said Mrs. Merton. "And Sybil would *love* to help you," she added.

Sybil picked up her plate and took it to the sink. She was not happy.

Mr. Merton *was* happy. It was his night to wash dishes. "I think I'll go read the newspaper," he said. "Or see what's on TV."

Howie turned on the water. He put lots of soap in the sink. The bubbles were the only good part of washing dishes. The countertop was piled high with plates and glasses. There were pots and pans, too.

Sybil looked at him suspiciously. "Why are you Mr. Volunteer all of a sudden?" she asked.

"I just want to help Mom and Dad," Howie said innocently. "After I do the dishes, I'm going to clean my room."

"Clean it? You should just declare it a national emergency and call in the National Guard," said Sybil.

Howie just smiled. . . .

"Is this really Howie's room?" asks Edith in a hushed voice. "It's spotless! Why, look! I can see myself!"

"Of course you can see yourself, Edith," says Magic Merton. "That's a mirror."

"Oh, Howie, you're so smart," sighs Edith.

"Howie!" cries Sybil. "I've dropped my hanky out the window."

"I'll just fly down and get it for you," says Magic Merton. He leaps gracefully out the window.

"I wish Howie Merton were *my* brother," says Edith.

"Howie! The sink is overflowing!" Sybil's voice brought Howie back to reality.

"Right," he said, turning off the faucet. "As soon as these are done, I'm tackling my room. No matter how long it takes. Because I'm a good kid."

"If you want to be a *great* kid, you can clean my room too," said Sybil.

Howie shook his head. "I said I was good, not crazy."

5

Week Three:

A Really Good Show and Tell

Howie waited six long days to hear from Eddie. Finally, on his way to school on the seventh day, he found a note on the toolshed door.

MAGIC TRAINEE ORDER #3

YOU WILL HELP LIONEL FIND SOMETHING REALLY GOOD FOR SHOW AND TELL. I WILL KNOW!!!!!!

Howie could not believe it. How did Eddie know about Lionel and show and tell? Her magic power was amazing!

Lionel was in the kitchen with Mrs. Ross when Howie and Roy got home from school. He was sitting at the table tossing grapes in the air and trying to catch them in his mouth.

Howie took two apples from the refrigerator and handed one to Roy. They sat down with Lionel to tell Mrs. Ross about their day at school.

"Sandra Sue Baker wore a bright pink dress today. With lots of ruffles," Howie said. "I'll bet it glows in the dark!" He took a big bite out of his apple. "She is the loudest, bossiest, most *awful* girl in my class."

"She's the most awful girl in the *world,*" said Roy.

"What's wrong with Sandra Sue?" Mrs. Ross asked.

"Howie doesn't like her because she's always scoring goals in soccer and he's the goalie," said Lionel.

"I don't care if she makes goals," Howie said. "But she tells everyone I let her make goals because I *like* her."

Roy nodded. "And Sandra Sue hates to lose."

"If Sandra Sue's team isn't winning, she changes the rules. If somebody gets the ball away from her, she says they kicked her and goes crying to the nurse's office. Girls don't play fair," Howie said.

"Not all girls are like Sandra Sue Baker,"

Mrs. Ross said. "My granddaughter Edwina plays a great second base."

Impossible, thought Howie. She's just another girl.

Howie took one last bite from his apple and then he pulled Lionel upstairs to their bedroom. Roy followed. "What are we doing, Howie?" Lionel asked.

"I'm going to help you find something really great for show and tell this week," Howie said.

"You're going to *help* me?" Lionel said. "Why?"

"Yeah," said Roy. "Why?"

"I already told you that I'm not giving you my new baseball card," said Lionel. "So it's no use being nice to me."

Howie didn't answer. He simply opened the door to the closet, pulled Lionel's desk inside, and climbed on top of it. When Howie stood up, he could reach the ceiling. Lionel watched as Howie slid open a small door. It was the door to the attic. Howie had seen his dad go up there.

Howie pulled himself up into the attic. He looked back down at Lionel. "Stand on the desk. I'll pull you up," he said.

Lionel stood on tiptoe. Howie pulled him

by the arm while Roy pushed from below.
Lionel reached for the door with his other
hand. Suddenly he was standing next to
Howie. "Neat!" he said, looking around at all
the boxes and trunks and strange old things.

Roy's head popped up through the trap-
door. "Yeah, neat!" he said. "Now I get it,"
he said, pulling himself up into the attic. "We
get to play with all this junk."

"No, we are really going to help Lionel find
something for show and tell," Howie said. He
picked up a cookie jar. It was shaped like a
cowboy's head. Howie took off the cowboy hat
lid and looked inside. No cookies. "Come on,"
he said.

"Sure," said Roy. He started looking too.

Lionel looked at everything. He looked at
a green lamp with a base like a cactus. It was
sitting on a three-legged table that tilted to
one side. "I don't know why Mom put this stuff
in the attic. It's great!" he said.

"How about this?" asked Roy, holding up a
stuffed bear that was missing an ear. Lionel
shook his head.

"Or this, Lionel?" Howie asked, pulling Mr.
Merton's army uniform out of a box. Lionel
shook his head again.

"Look at that," Roy said, pointing to a little Christmas tree made out of shiny blue aluminum. Lionel didn't even answer.

Howie pulled out books and pictures. Roy pulled out skis and ice skates. Lionel just kept shaking his head. Howie and Roy gave up. They sat down on a big box and waited as

Lionel worked his way through everything in the attic.

Finally he held up a big pink pillow with purple fringe and a picture of a smiling alligator on it.

"What does it say?" he asked.

"Souvenir of Florida," read Howie. "A souvenir is something you buy when you're on vacation," he explained.

"An alligator is bigger than a snakeskin, and it could eat Gloria Nicks's coyote in one big bite. This is it! It's perfect for show and tell," Lionel said.

"All right!" Howie shouted. Howie and Roy jumped off the box. They didn't want to give Lionel the chance to change his mind. They helped Lionel down and then handed him the pillow.

Howie, Lionel, and Roy took the pillow to the kitchen. "Mrs. Ross," said Lionel, "look at the pillow I found for show and tell!" He plumped the pillow and clouds of dust rose out of it. Howie and Roy started to cough. "Howie helped me find it," Lionel said.

Mrs. Ross waved away the dust and took a closer look. "I'll bet kindergarten has never seen anything like it!" she said.

"That's what I think!" said Lionel happily.

Mrs. Ross began to laugh. "I'll have to re-member to tell Edwina about this," she said.

The boys carried the pillow out to the backyard. Lionel wanted to show Sybil. She was standing on her head, as usual.

Howie and Lionel held the pillow upside down so that she could see it.

"Why is the alligator smiling?" asked Sybil.

"Because it just ate a girl who stands on her head and asks dumb questions," said Howie.

Mrs. Merton's car pulled into the driveway. They showed her the pillow too.

"Oh, Lionel," she said. "Where did you find that?"

"In the attic," Lionel said.

"You climbed into the attic all by yourself?"

"Howie helped me," said Lionel.

"You didn't give Howie your baseball cards, did you?" asked Mrs. Merton.

Lionel shook his head. "He wanted to help me."

Mrs. Merton got out of the car. "First you do the dishes," she said to Howie. "Then you clean your room. Now you're helping your brother. What's next?" she asked. . . .

"Here's Howie's report card, Mrs. Merton," says Ms. Jackson. "You can see that it is perfect in every way."

"All A's!" says Mrs. Merton. "And he never has to study. It's like—"

"Magic?" says Ms. Jackson. "That's what we think, too. Why, if there's a word that I can't spell, I just ask Howie. He's a walking dictionary."

Magic, thought Howie. That's what's next.

6

Week Four:
Sandra Sue Baker

It was a cold, foggy day. Howie walked to the toolshed. It had been four days since he had followed his last magic trainee order. He wanted to see if there was a new note.

"Hi!" Eddie said, stepping out from behind the shed.

Howie jumped. "Don't scare me like that!" he said.

Eddie smiled. "You've been a great magic trainee, Howie," she said. "Thanks to you, Lionel was a show-and-tell star. The class really liked that smiling alligator."

Wow! thought Howie. That is exactly what Lionel said when he came home from school. Eddie knows everything! Being magic is going to be great!

Eddie pulled a note out of her baggy jeans.

She folded it and gave it to him. "Don't read it yet!" she said. "Wait until I'm gone!" She walked just a few steps and the fog closed in. She disappeared.

Howie opened the note. It said:

MAGIC TRAINEE ORDER #4

THE MAGIC TRAINEE MUST WALK HOME FROM SCHOOL WITH SANDRA SUE BAKER.

Howie couldn't believe it. He read the note twice. Then he crumpled it up and threw it as hard as he could. "Eddie!" he shouted. "Eddie!" But there was no answer.

How did Eddie know about Sandra Sue Baker? Sandra Sue was much worse than fish heads or washing the dishes or cleaning his room. "Not Sandra Sue! I won't!" groaned Howie. But somehow he knew he would. He had to. He tried not to think about what might happen if he didn't finish his training. . . .

"Here's another Christmas present for Howie," says Mrs. Merton.

"Is it more socks and underwear?" asks Sybil. "Or maybe a tie this time?"

"I thought about buying him a walkie-talkie," says Mr. Merton. "Then for some strange reason I changed my mind. I decided to get him a math workbook instead."

Walking home with Sandra Sue was his last trainee order. To be magic he had to do it. But it wasn't going to be easy.

On Monday, Roy wanted to play softball. Howie had to say yes. There was no way he could tell Roy he couldn't play because he had to walk a girl home from school. On Tuesday, Sandra Sue wore her glow-in-the-dark dress. Howie would not be seen with a girl who wore a dress like that. On Wednesday, Sandra Sue went to her Girl Scout meeting.

On Thursday, Howie sat in class with his head in his hands. Time was running out. He did not want to think about Eddie or magic dust. He didn't want to think about Sandra Sue Baker, either. Instead he listened to the teacher. Ms. Jackson was asking for a helper.

"Sandra Sue has let us all share her gerbil, but now it's time for the gerbil to go back home to Sandra Sue's house. Is there someone who can carry its cage and its food? Someone who can walk Sandra Sue and her gerbil all the way home?"

This is it, thought Howie. He jumped up. *"Me!"* he shouted. "I'll do it!"

Everyone in class turned to look at Howie, including Roy. "Howie!" said Roy. "Sit down! Are you nuts? It's Sandra Sue!"

"Howie, if you want to help so *much,"* said Ms. Jackson, frowning at Roy, "you may walk Sandra Sue home."

Howie sat down. He did not know whether to be happy or sick. He was one step closer to magic. He was also eight long blocks from Sandra Sue Baker's house.

"Careful with that cage," Sandra Sue said as she and Howie started down the hall after school.

"Don't get bossy, Sandra Sue," Howie told her. "I just have to walk you home. I don't have to take orders."

Sandra Sue pouted. "I don't know why you wanted to carry Sweetykins home anyway."

"Sweetykins?"

"That's my gerbil's name," said Sandra Sue.

Howie made a gagging noise. He was really earning his magic dust the hard way.

"Come on," Sandra Sue said, pulling on

Howie's arm. "I've got to get home. I have a
piano lesson."

Howie trudged along a few steps behind her.
"Don't hold the cage like that," she said.

"You have to keep it level so Sweetykins doesn't lose his balance."

Howie sighed and shifted the cage.

"Not like that," said Sandra Sue. "Sweetykins doesn't like your hand to be on the side of the cage. It scares him."

"What else can I do?" Howie asked. "Carry it on my head?"

"I didn't want you to carry it at all," Sandra Sue told him. "In fact, I wanted anyone *but* you to carry Sweetykins's cage. Why are you doing this?" she asked.

"What if I told you I was a magic trainee?" said Howie. "And that I have to do all kinds of terrible things—like fall in a pile of fish heads and walk home with dorky girls who cheat at soccer before I get my own magic powers?"

"Oh, right!" snorted Sandra Sue. "You think that everyone believes those dumb stories of yours, Howie Merton. Well, I don't. They are all lies! So there!"

Howie smiled. "Here, kitty, kitty, kitty," he said softly as they turned onto Sandra Sue's block. "Where are you, little ghost kitty?"

Sandra Sue looked around. "You aren't calling that cat ghost, are you?" she asked.

"I thought you didn't believe in cat ghosts," Howie said.

Sandra Sue frowned. "I *don't!* I just don't want any cats around my Sweetykins," she said.

"Take it easy," Howie said. "Cat ghosts don't eat gerbils."

"Good," said Sandra Sue.

"Cat ghosts eat people," said Howie.

"Howie Merton, you stop that!" said Sandra Sue.

"Actually they don't eat all people—just girls."

"That's not funny!" Sandra Sue yelled as she ran for her front door. She pounded on the door until Mrs. Baker opened it.

"Sandra Sue, what's the matter?" asked her mother.

"Howie Merton has a cat ghost!" Sandra Sue said as she pushed past Mrs. Baker.

Mrs. Baker looked down at Howie, who was standing on the front porch. "What's this about a cat ghost?" she asked.

Howie gave Mrs. Baker the cage. "It looks like a gerbil to me, Mrs. Baker," he said. Then he turned and leaped for joy off the Bakers' front porch. The worst was over.

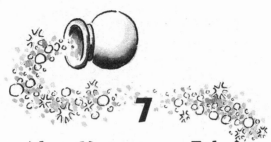

7

Also Known as Edwina

Howie could not wait to see Eddie. He had carried fish heads, washed dishes, cleaned his room, helped Lionel find the perfect show and tell, and walked home with Sandra Sue Baker. He had done it all. Now Eddie would sprinkle him with magic dust, and he would be magic forever.

Howie checked the toolshed door first thing Saturday morning. He was hoping for a note, but he was hoping even more to find Eddie. But there was no note and no Eddie.

After church on Sunday morning, Howie ran to the toolshed only to be disappointed all over again. Where was she?

In school on Monday, Howie thought about studying the spelling words for the week. He took a long look at the list and decided to forget it. Why waste time on spelling words? Eddie might be waiting for him at that very moment. . . .

"Just get on your knees and I'll sprinkle the magic dust over your head," says Eddie. "I never know how much to use. Some people don't need a lot. They have natural magical talent. For others I have to use buckets of the stuff."

Eddie sprinkles a pinch of magic dust over his head. "Now," says Eddie, "spell Mississippi."

"M-i-s-s-i-s-s-i-p-p-i," says Howie.

"Wow!" says Eddie. "This is incredible. You're the best magic trainee I've ever had."

There was no sign of Eddie on Tuesday. By Wednesday, Howie was worried. By Thursday, he was frantic. By Friday, he had flunked another spelling test. By Saturday, he was depressed.

Howie sat at the kitchen table with his head in his hands. Mrs. Ross was cutting carrots and potatoes into a big pot. "You look like you need a friend, Howie," she said. "Did I tell you my granddaughter Edwina is in town?"

"Is she on vacation?" Howie asked.

"No. She lives with her father on his boat. Whenever they dock, she comes to visit me."

"Doesn't she go to school?" he asked.

"No. I pick up her assignments from school and give them to her. She studies while she's at sea. When she visits me, she brings me her work. She does the same work that you do."

"She's lucky," said Howie. "No tests, no reading groups—"

"No recess, no friends," finished Mrs. Ross. "As I was saying, Edwina's in town this afternoon. She's over at my house. I've told her so much about you. Why don't you go over and surprise her?"

"I don't know her," said Howie. "And anyway, I don't play with girls."

"What, may I ask, is wrong with girls?"

Howie turned around. His mother stood in the doorway. "I think girls are smart, interesting, and fun," she said. "I happen to be a girl myself."

"You're not a girl. You're my mother," Howie said.

"I had to start somewhere," said Mrs. Merton. "Why don't *you* start by going over to meet Edwina?"

"Why?" he asked.

"You can never have too many friends."

Howie sighed and stood up. He didn't feel like arguing.

"Cheer up," said Mrs. Ross. "Edwina is a lot of fun. Not at all like Sandra Sue Baker."

Howie slowly climbed Mrs. Ross's front steps and pressed the doorbell. He waited and then pressed it again. The door swung open. A girl with long blond hair stood there. "All right, all right, don't wear it out—" She stopped and stared at Howie.

Howie stared back at her. Right into her green eyes. It was Eddie.

"What are *you* doing here?" Howie asked. "I came to see Edwina." And then suddenly he knew. It all made sense. "You're Edwina, aren't you?" Howie's face turned red. "You . . . you . . . liar!" he shouted.

"I am not a liar, Howie Merton! You take that back!"

"Sure you knew what we had for dinner. Your grandmother cooked it! And you didn't need magic to know about the cat ghost *or* show and tell *or* Sandra Sue. There's no magic, is there? It was all a trick!"

"What about *your* trick, Howie Merton?"

Eddie asked. "You told all those kids that there was a cat ghost in your toolshed."

"I just made up that story for fun."

"A made-up story is a lie," said Eddie. "You're just mad because I didn't believe your story and you believed mine! Besides, I told you the truth."

"No, you didn't! You said I could get the spelling words right! Every week!" said Howie.

"Well, you can. All you have to do is study."

Howie couldn't believe his ears. "What about Santa? You said I could talk to Santa!"

"You *can* talk to Santa," Eddie said. "He's at Smith's Department Store every Saturday from Thanksgiving until Christmas."

"You said I would be magic." Howie was so angry his voice cracked.

"I didn't say you would *be* magic. I said you could join the Magic Club," said Eddie. There were tears in her eyes.

Howie turned and started for home. He needed to think. He didn't lie! A made-up story wasn't a lie. Or at least he didn't think it was. Suddenly he wasn't sure about anything. Eddie had definitely lied to him, but Howie had to admit she was very smart. However, he was not going to forgive her. Ever.

He began to run. He reached the back door and yanked it open. He burst into the kitchen just as Mrs. Ross was putting on her coat. "Back so soon?" she asked him. "Was Edwina surprised? Are you two playing a game?"

Howie pulled off his coat and threw it onto a chair. "Yeah, we were playing a game," he said. "And I lost."

8

Friends Are Magic People

After church the next morning, Howie changed into his play clothes. He couldn't go outside because it was raining. He looked out at the soggy backyard. He thought back to the first day that he met Eddie. She had been leaning on the toolshed door. The door! There was something on the door. Howie could see it blowing in the wind.

"Lunch will be ready in a minute," called Mrs. Merton as Howie raced by, pulling on his jacket.

"Be right back," he shouted.

There was a small plastic bag pinned to the door. Inside the bag was a note. It was from Eddie. Howie walked back to the house holding the bag. Maybe he would not even open it. Why should he? Eddie had made him feel like a stupid little kid.

Howie wanted to rip up the note and throw it away. But he didn't. He missed Eddie. There hadn't been much to do in Port Amblin before she came along. He read the note.

Howie,

I'm really sorry. I didn't mean to hurt your feelings. I just wanted to be your friend. I liked my grandma's stories about you. Everything you did sounded like fun. I knew that the cat ghost was a made-up story. I didn't think you would mind if I made up a story, too. I know we probably can't be friends. But if we can, meet our boat. We'll be back at the dock at noon on Saturday. I probably won't see you.

Eddie

Howie folded the note and put it in his pocket. Saturday was a long time from Sunday. He didn't have to decide right now. He was going to eat lunch and think about Eddie some other time.

It was still raining on Monday morning. Howie sat and looked at the spelling words on the blackboard. He wrote the words in his spelling notebook. On the edge of the paper he drew a picture of a boat. He drew water all around the boat. He drew a girl standing on the boat and then he drew a dock. There was no one standing on the dock.

The rain stopped on Tuesday. There were gray clouds in the sky. Howie walked home from school by himself. Roy was out sick with a sore throat. Howie walked with his head down. When he stopped and looked up, he was in front of Mrs. Ross's house. Howie walked to the door and rang the doorbell.

"I'm glad to see you, Howie," said Mrs. Ross. She gave him a hug. "Come in." Howie walked into her kitchen. Eddie's friend Thomas was sitting at the table drinking a cup of coffee. Thomas smiled at him.

"Hello there, Howie," Thomas said. "Have a seat." Howie sat, and Mrs. Ross put a glass of milk and a plate of cookies in front of him.

"Do you want to talk about it?" she asked him.

"There is nothing to talk about," said Howie. Miss Marshmallow rubbed against his legs and made a soft cat sound.

"Edwina told me the story. She said she played a trick on you. Is that right?" Mrs. Ross looked at Howie over the top of her glasses.

Howie nodded. He patted Miss Marshmallow on the head.

"I didn't know that you actually believed Eddie's 'magic' story," Thomas said. "I thought you two were just playing a game."

"Eddie was playing a game," Howie said. "I wasn't."

"She told me that she was sorry," Mrs. Ross said. "Did she tell you that she was sorry?"

Howie nodded again.

"Eddie would really like to have a friend. I have a feeling you could use a friend, too." Mrs. Ross smiled. "A friend who is not afraid of cat ghosts."

"Tricking someone is no way to be a friend," Howie said. He looked at Thomas.

Mrs. Ross picked up Howie's empty plate and carried it to the sink. "Maybe it wasn't a good idea, but why not give her another chance? Think about it," she said.

Wednesday was still cloudy. Howie took the practice spelling test. He missed six words out of ten. He looked at the paper and thought about what Eddie had said about spelling words.

The sun was shining on Thursday. Howie shot baskets after school. He thought about Eddie and all the crazy things he had done to be magic. "She *did* lie," Howie said to himself. "I'm not good at spelling. I couldn't get all the words right just by studying." Then he had an idea. "I'll show her. I'll prove that she lied." Howie went into the house. He found his backpack in the kitchen. He dug through it until he found his spelling words. Then he took them into the living room to study.

Sybil and Edith were there. Sybil was standing on her head. "What are you doing?" Edith asked Howie.

Howie sat down with his books. "Studying," he said.

Sybil and Edith burst out laughing. "No, really," Edith said. "What are you doing?"

"Studying," Howie said again.

Sybil was so surprised she fell over. "Who are you and what have you done with the real Howie Merton?" she cried.

Howie didn't even look up. He was too busy copying out the spelling words.

Spelling was always first on Friday, right after the Pledge of Allegiance. Ms. Jackson said each spelling word slowly and gave the students time to write. Howie carefully wrote each word. When the test was over, Ms. Jackson picked up the papers.

"Class, open your reading books," Ms. Jackson said. She sat down at her desk and began to correct the spelling tests. Howie tried to read. He looked up at Ms. Jackson. She was using her red pencil. He looked back at his book.

Then Ms. Jackson stood up and walked over to the spelling chart. Everyone who got all

ten words right got a gold star. Ms. Jackson
put a gold star by Sandra Sue's name. Sandra
Sue looked smug. She always got a gold star.
Ms. Jackson put four more gold stars on the
chart. Then she put a gold star next to Howie's
name.

Sandra Sue leaned over to him. "What did
you do? Cheat?" she whispered.

"It was magic," Howie said.

Howie got up early on Saturday morning to
help his dad work in the yard. Mr. Merton
showed Howie how to trim the bushes. Mr.
Merton knew all about which branches to cut
off the trees, too. Howie thought his dad was
really smart. As they put away the lawn
mower he asked, "Dad, do you believe in
magic?"

Mr. Merton smiled. "I had a magic kit when
I was your age," he said. "I could make hoops
go together and then come apart. I could make
the ace of hearts jump right out of the deck.
It was great."

"Was it really magic?" Howie asked. "Or was
it just a trick?"

"Magic is always a trick," said Mr. Merton.
"It becomes real when someone believes in
it."

"Do you believe in it?"

"I'd hate to be one of those people who doesn't believe in magic," said Mr. Merton. "Know what I mean?"

Howie nodded. Suddenly he felt happy. "I have to go see someone," he said. "I'll be back in an hour." He ran out of the yard, down to Main Street, and over to Bartlett Street. He ran down the alley behind Watson's Pretty Fine Fish, all the way to the docks.

A boat with the name *Edwina* painted on its side was bobbing up and down in the water. A man was working at the ropes. Eddie stood nearby, watching him.

"Eddie! Hey, *Eddie!*" Howie shouted, waving.

Eddie looked at Howie. Then she leaned down and said something to her father. He nodded. She jumped from the boat to the dock and ran over to Howie. "You did come," she said.

"I just thought I'd tell you that I studied my spelling words. And you were right. I got a gold star."

Eddie grinned. "I was? You did?"

"I thought I'd tell you that." Howie stuffed his hands into his pockets. He didn't know what else to say.

Eddie waited.

"Do you want to help me and Roy?" Howie finally blurted out. "We're going to paint big red cat-paw prints all over the toolshed next week."

Eddie nodded. "As long as you're here, do you want to meet my dad?" she asked.

"Sure," Howie said. They ran back to the boat.

"Hey, Dad," Eddie said. Mr. Ross looked up from his work. He had green eyes just like Eddie's.

"Who's this?" he asked his daughter.

"It's Howie," Eddie said. "My friend."

About the Author

"There really was a cat skeleton behind our toolshed when I was a child," says FAYE COUCH REEVES. "It scared all the children in the neighborhood—and inspired me to write about Howie." Faye Couch Reeves lives in Albuquerque, New Mexico, with her husband and two daughters. *Howie Merton and the Magic Dust* is her first book for children.

About the Illustrator

JON BULLER has written and illustrated many books for children, often teaming up with Susan Schade, his wife. Their collaborations include *No Tooth, No Quarter!* and *The Noisy Counting Book.* They live in Lyme, Connecticut.